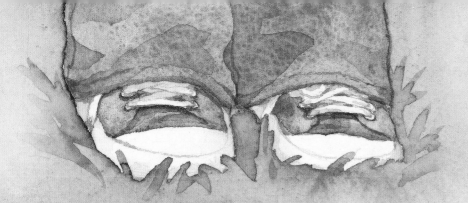

One Tractor

by **Alexandra Siy**

illustrated by
Jacqueline Rogers

I Like to Read®

HOLIDAY HOUSE • NEW YORK

I Like to Read® books, created by award-winning
picture book artists as well as talented newcomers,
instill confidence and the joy of reading in new readers.

We want to hear every new reader say, "I like to read!"

_____

Visit our website for flash cards, activities, and more about the series:
www.holidayhouse.com/ILiketoRead
#ILTR
This book has been tested by an educational expert
and determined to be a guided reading level G.

I LIKE TO READ is a registered trademark of Holiday House Publishing, Inc.
Originally published in 2008 as One Tractor: A Counting Book.

Text copyright © 2008 by Alexandra Siy
Illustrations copyright © 2008 by Jacqueline Rogers
All Rights Reserved
HOLIDAY HOUSE is registered in the U.S. Patent and Trademark Office.
Printed and bound in November 2017 at Toppan Leefung, DongGuan City, China.
The artwork for this book was created with watercolors.
www.holidayhouse.com
3 5 7 9 10 8 6 4

Library of Congress Cataloging-in-Publication Data
Siy, Alexandra.
One tractor: a counting book / by Alexandra Siy;
illustrated by Jacqueline Rogers.—1st ed.
p. cm.
Summary: While one tractor sits on the grass, out of gas, increasing numbers of other vehicles,
from two airplanes to ten bicycles, fill the backyard with adventure.
ISBN-13: 978-0-8234-1923-4 (hardcover)
ISBN-10: 0-8234-1923-1 (hardcover)
[I. Vehicles—Fiction. 2. Counting. 3. Stories in rhyme.]
I. Rogers, Jacqueline, 1958— ill. II. Title.
PZ8.3.S6183One 2008
[E]—dc22
2006101431
ISBN 978-0-8234-4015-3 (ILTR paperback)

To Leo, who likes tractors
A. S.

For Ben Tassinari
1976–2007

With special thanks to my models:
Jacob Mesick (for the jacket pose),
Sam Reilly (for the hairstyle),
and Evan Warkov (whom I kept thinking
about while I painted these pictures).
J. R.

One tractor
in the grass,
out of gas.

Two planes
fly in the sky,
small plane low,
big plane high.

Three boats
float below

sailing fast,
docking slow.

Four cranes
above the town

hoist it up,
easy down.

Five big trucks
ready to pull,

one empty,
the others full.

Six city buses,
right bus,
wrong . . .

stopping,
going, all day long.

Seven fire trucks
aim cold spray,
hosing red-hot flames away.

Eight machines

shovel,

dump,

push,

scrape,

dig,

roll,

doze,

load!

Turning rough earth
into smooth, black road.

Nine railroad cars
speed under the ground,

now over a bridge
into sunlight and sound.

Ten bicycles
locked in the rack,

headlights in front,
baskets in back.

One tractor
in the grass,
out of gas.

Suddenly, Lion felt very homesick. He missed his friends and the hot grasslands of Africa. "I want to go home," he roared.

"I miss fresh bamboo shoots from China," said Panda.

"I miss the hot, sunny desert of Australia," said Emu.

"I miss the cold snow of the North Pole," said Polar Bear.

"I want to go home to Africa with Lion," said Monkey.

But then Monkey had an idea.

"Don't worry, everyone," he said, and quietly he stretched out his long arms and unhooked the keys from zoo keeper Sam's belt. In a flash, Monkey unlocked all the cages.

The animals tiptoed out of the zoo

and onto the bus.

At the port, they met Wise Bird.
"Hello! What are you doing out here?" she asked.
"We're going home," said Lion. "Can you show us the way?"
Wise Bird showed them four ships that were about to leave
for Africa, China, Australia, and the North Pole.
"All aboard!" called the captains.

"All aboard!"

"We'll miss you!" said Lion
and Monkey. They gave
everyone a big hug and
boarded the ship to Africa.
Panda got on the ship to
China, Emu got on the ship to
Australia, and Polar Bear got
on the one to the North Pole.
"Good-bye!" they all called.

Soon Lion and Monkey were sailing home, far away from the zoo and their friends. Days passed. Monkey dreamed of swinging in the trees. Lion dreamed of the sweet smell of the grassland baking in the sun.

Then, one night, the smell was so strong it made Lion's nose twitch and woke him up. He peered over the edge of the boat and saw land. "Monkey, wake up!" he cried. "We're home!"

On the shore, Lion and Monkey's friends
were waiting.
"Hooray!" the friends cried. "You're home!"
They made Lion and Monkey a delicious supper
and told them all the news. Lion and Monkey told
their friends about the zoo and their exciting escape.

The next day, Lion and Monkey
ate their favorite foods for breakfast,
bathed in their favorite waterhole,
ate something scrumptious for lunch,
played their favorite game of hide-and-seek,
and slept outside under the moon and the stars.

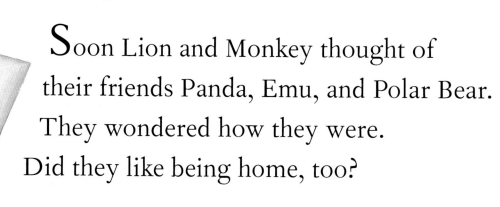

Soon Lion and Monkey thought of their friends Panda, Emu, and Polar Bear. They wondered how they were. Did they like being home, too?

Then one day, Wise Bird came to visit. She was carrying a beakful of postcards. Lion and Monkey jumped up and down with excitement. Lion read the first one:

Dear friends,
I arrived home safely. The fresh bamboo shoots are delicious.
It's good to be back with my family.
I even have a new nephew. Isn't he sweet?
Maybe you can come and visit sometime?
I miss you, but I am glad to be home.
Love from Panda

Monkey read the second postcard:

Hello, old chums,
Cool at last! The snow is
wonderful. Here's a picture of
my favorite fishing place. Look what
I caught for my dinner! Sea Lion is my
new friend. He's good at fishing, too!
I miss you both. Please write soon.
Love from Polar Bear

T he third postcard was from Emu:

Hi, there!
I'm home at last, and I've made
a new friend called Kangaroo.
Here's a photo of her. We have fun
exploring the desert together. Kangaroo and
I like to race across the sand. Don't tell her
I told you, but I nearly always beat her!
I miss you and will always remember our
exciting escape from the zoo.
Love from Emu

Lion and Monkey were so happy to hear from their friends! They decided to write back to Panda, Emu, and Polar Bear.

Why don't you send a postcard, too?